All the Way to the Stars

Annalena McAfee
and Anthony Lewis

RED FOX

A Red Fox Book

Published by Random House Children's Books
20 Vauxhall Bridge Road, London SW1V 2SA

A division of Random House UK Ltd
London Melbourne Sydney Auckland
Johannesburg and agencies throughout the world

3 5 7 9 10 8 6 4 2

First published in Great Britain by Julia MacRae 1995
Red Fox edition 1999

Printed in Hong Kong

RANDOM HOUSE UK Limited Reg. No. 954009

ISBN 0 09 944241 8

I've had a lot of birthdays,

I even go to school.
I ride my bike all on my own

and like to help around the house.

But every day my mummy says,

When I'm big...

I'll eat all the sweets in the sweetshop

and ride a really huge bike.

When I'm a big boy
I'll teach my teacher,
and send my mummy
to bed early for being naughty.

I'll drive a big red bus
to the seaside,

go on every ride at the funfair,
and no-one will ever say,
"Don't do that!
That's for big boys!"

I'll visit the zoo and join the monkeys for tea.

I'll have a pet pig and take him for walks in the woods.

When I'm a big boy, I'll sail a ship
to the top and bottom of the world

to see the koalas in Australia,

the tigers in India,

the bears in Alaska,

and the penguins in Antarctica.

I'll find heaps of buried treasure
when I'm a big boy,
and fight off silly pirates,

and keep a parrot
that sings rude songs.

When I'm a big boy
I'll fly a plane
all the way to the stars.

And make sandcastles on the moon.

But I'll still come home
to play with my toys

and see my mummy.